CONFLICT IN EASTERN EUROPE

Bernard Harbor

New York

Conflicts

Titles in the series:
The Breakup of the Soviet Union
Conflict in Eastern Europe
Conflict in the Middle East
Conflict in Southern Africa

Cover: The Berlin Wall was erected in 1961 by the East German government to prevent East Germans moving to the West. Until its destruction, following the revolution of 1989, it was a powerful symbol of the division of Europe. Here, West Germans are seen scaling the wall on November 9, 1989.

Title page: Bucharest, June 19, 1991: workers protesting against Ion Iliescu's National Salvation Front government. (See box on page 34.)

Picture acknowledgments
The publishers would like to thank the following for supplying their photographs for use as illustrations in this book:
Camera Press Ltd 10 (Felix Aeberli), 11 (Erma), 19 (MTI), 22 (MTI), 25 (R. Mildenhall), 31 (Erma), 33 (Piotr Malecki), 34 (CAF), 36 (Jutka Rona), 39 (Beryl Sokoloff); David Cumming 23; Eye Ubiquitous 18; Impact 27 (David Stewart-Smith), 37 (John Cole); Popperfoto 5, 40 (AFP), 41 (AFP), 44; Rex Features *Cover* (Jacques Witt/Sipa), 4 (Sichov), 13 (Alfred), 14 (Girod), 15 (Peter Brooker), 17, 20 (Facelly/Sipa), 24 (Schroeder and Seneport/Sipa), 26 (CTK/Sipa), 29 (Malanca/Sipa), 32 (Tom Haley/Sipa), 45 (Craig Easton); Topham Picture Source *Title page* (Siumui Chan/str), 7, 8, 9 (Associated Press), 12 (Associated Press), 16, 21 (Siumui Chan/str), 28 (Luca Turi/str), 30 (Universal Pictorial Press), 35 (Associated Press), 38 (Associated Press), 43 (Jim James/PJ).
The maps on pages 6 and 42 were supplied by Peter Bull.

Editor: Roger Coote
Series editor: William Wharfe
Consultant: Dr. Martyn Rady, Lecturer in Central European History,
    School of Slavonic and East European Studies, University of London
Designer/Typesetter: Malcolm Walker/Kudos Editorial and Design Services

First American publication 1993 by New Discovery Books, Macmillan Publishing Company, 866 Third Avenue, New York, NY 10022

Macmillan Publishing Company is part of the Maxwell Communication Group of Companies

First published in 1993 by Wayland (Publishers) Ltd, 61 Western Road, Hove, East Sussex BN3 1JD

Library of Congress Cataloging-in-Publication Data

Harbor, Bernard, 1960–
    Conflict in Eastern Europe /Bernard Harbor.
        p. cm. — (Conflicts)
    Includes bibliographical references (p.) and index.
    Summary: The recent tumultuous events and the rise and fall of
    Communism are described here.
    ISBN 0-02-742626-2
    1. Europe, Eastern—History—1989– —Juvenile literature.
    I. Title. II. Series.
    DJK51.H37 1993
    947—dc20   93-3035

Printed in Italy by G. Canale & C. S. p. A., Turin

Contents

CHANGE AND CONFLICT

Although revolutions are usually associated with violence, most of those that took place in the Eastern European countries between 1989 and 1991 were surprisingly peaceful. Very few lives were lost when the seemingly immovable power of the Eastern European Communist regimes was swept away, especially in comparison to other examples of rapid political change throughout the world.

Conflict takes many forms, however. Even when lives are not lost and physical injuries are not sustained, different forms of conflict arise. The changes in Eastern Europe, from Communist control to multiparty democracy and from the command economy to the free market, could not have been more extreme. Yet they happened in a very short time. As a result, political, economic, religious, and ethnic conflicts arose. In the case of Yugoslavia, these conflicts led to a vicious civil war in which many people were killed and injured.

This book looks at the various conflicts that arose across Eastern Europe as a result of the sudden economic and political changes that took place in the late 1980s and early 1990s. It was a time of new opportunities and new challenges. Optimists looked forward to a rebirth of cultural

A crowd of East and West Germans celebrating the opening of the Berlin Wall on November 9, 1989

New conflicts soon arose from the ashes of Eastern European Communism. Yugoslavia descended into bloody civil war. This picture shows a Bosnian militiaman in Sarajevo in May 1992.

and economic life in the region. But the emerging democracies had to deal with new conflicts, as well as those hitherto frozen by forty years of Soviet dominance and rigid Communist rule.

The following chapters look at the problems that arose and the solutions that were attempted (with varying degrees of success) by the new governments of Eastern Europe. They tell the story of a particular region, but they also relate to the wider story of the greatest political conflict of the 20th century—that between the conflicting systems of capitalism and multiparty democracy on the one hand and Communism on the other.

HISTORY AND GEOGRAPHY

Following the end of World War II in 1945, the term *Eastern Europe* was applied to eight countries—Albania, Bulgaria, Czechoslovakia, East Germany, Hungary, Poland, Romania, and Yugoslavia. Although some of these countries shared a cultural, ethnic, and historical experience, the idea of Eastern Europe was essentially a political definition used to describe the European countries that were allied to the Soviet Union or had Communist governments.

In fact, the countries of Eastern Europe, which stretched from the Baltic Sea in the north to the Mediterranean in the south and from the border of West Germany and Austria in the west to the Soviet border in the east, had at least as many differences as they had similarities. Some, such as Hungary, Czechoslovakia, and East Germany, were essentially central European countries bordering Western countries with which they had a shared history. Others, including Romania and Bulgaria in the east, had more in common with their neighbors in the Soviet Union, especially in terms of their economic problems. In the south, Yugoslavia had as much in common with its Mediterranean neighbors as it did with Poland.

The countries were brought together as part of the settlement made between the victorious Allies after World War II. At a series of meetings in 1945 (the most important of which were held at Yalta and Potsdam), the United States, the Soviet Union, and Britain agreed on a basis for the division of power and influence in Europe. The Western

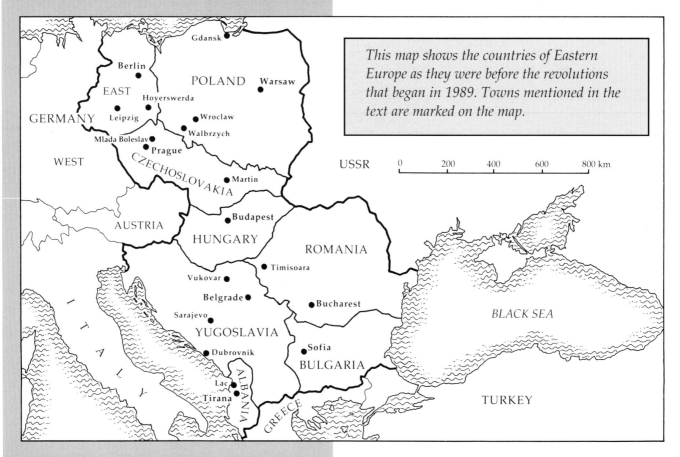

This map shows the countries of Eastern Europe as they were before the revolutions that began in 1989. Towns mentioned in the text are marked on the map.

The Baltic city of Danzig in 1921. After World War I, Danzig was declared a "free city" in which it was hoped its citizens—a mixture of Germans and Poles—could live together in peace. The city came under German control when it was invaded during World War II. After the war, it became part of Poland and today it is called Gdansk—the city in which Lech Walesa and Solidarność first challenged the Polish Communist authorities in 1980.

European states came under the political and economic influence of the United States and had parliamentary democracies and capitalist market economies. The Eastern European countries were to be under Soviet influence with Communist rule and command economies.

The division was in many ways arbitrary and had more to do with the location of Soviet and American forces at the end of the war than with anything else. Thus, Germany was literally split down the middle, with streets, families, and even houses cut in two by the division. Austria became nonaligned (in 1955) while its central European neighbors Czechoslovakia and Hungary were in the Eastern bloc.

During the 1950s and 1960s, hostilities among the Communist countries and the capitalist countries of the West grew worse and worse, developing into the cold war. The cold war meant that relations between East and West were at an all-time low, but war did not break out partly because of the threat of nuclear weapons, which both sides possessed.

Soviet influence

Although the Eastern European countries had their own individual economic and political features, their military, political, and economic affairs were almost totally dominated by the Soviet Union. Only Yugoslavia and Albania were formally independent of Soviet control.

Economic relations between the countries were regulated by the COMECON agreement, which governed trade between the countries. The Soviet Union had far greater natural resources than any of the other Communist countries and was able to sell raw materials and other products to the Eastern Europeans at low prices, in exchange for political obedience.

Military affairs, which were all-important during the cold war, were organized by the Warsaw Treaty Organization (or Warsaw Pact), which was also dominated by the Soviet Union. All Eastern European countries, except Yugoslavia and Albania (which withdrew in 1968), were members of the Warsaw Pact. Soviet troops were based in a number of Eastern European countries, including East Germany, Poland, and Czechoslovakia.

Any opposition to the Communist governments in Eastern Europe was suppressed by the military and the internal security forces—the secret police. Similarly, no criticism of the Soviet Union was tolerated. No independent political parties were allowed, and the Communists controlled all forms of public life. The only exception, in a few countries, was the Church. Officially, the Eastern European countries were atheistic, but some allowed a limited amount of religious activity. The Catholic church in Poland and the Protestant churches in East Germany

thus became a focus for opposition to Communism. The media and the arts were routinely subjected to censorship and any criticism of the Communist rulers, no matter how mild, was severely punished. This ruthless suppression of dissent was demonstrated most graphically by the Soviet-led military invasions of Hungary (1956) and Czechoslovakia (1968), carried out in response to political reforms of which the Soviet Union disapproved.

Discontent with the lack of political freedoms in Eastern Europe was matched only by dissatisfaction with daily economic life. Unlike the capitalist economies, Communism guaranteed the people of Eastern Europe a job and basic housing. The state also provided education, transportation, and health services. But the Communist economies were weak and inefficient compared to the industrialized countries in the West. Although life's essentials were readily available to most Eastern Europeans, consumers had little choice and few luxuries. Many longed for the higher standard of living enjoyed by many of their fellow Europeans in the West.

The Gorbachev revolution

In 1985, President Gorbachev came to power in the Soviet Union and instigated a dramatic program of political and economic reforms that were to change the face of the Soviet Union and Eastern Europe. He gradually introduced more

In 1968, Warsaw Pact troops invaded Czechoslovakia. This picture shows Czech citizens demonstrating against the invasion.

President Mikhail Gorbachev addressing the Soviet Parliament in 1989. He wanted to preserve Communism by reforming it. However, his reluctance to intervene in the Eastern European revolutions of 1989-1991 enabled democratic movements to overthrow Communism throughout the region. The fall of Communism also meant the end of Soviet influence, which had shaped Eastern Europe since 1945.

political freedoms and moved the failing Soviet economy closer and closer to a Western-style market economy.

Gorbachev's reforms affected Eastern Europe in two ways. First of all, Eastern Europeans saw the political reforms taking place in the Soviet Union and were encouraged to voice more loudly their own demands for change.

Second, partly because of a change in Soviet foreign policy and partly because of economic pressures, Gorbachev loosened the Soviet ties on the rest of Eastern Europe. He let it be known that

the Soviet Union would not intervene to prevent political change as it had in the past. Furthermore, the COMECON economic arrangements were loosened, too. The first point meant that change was possible; the second made change essential.

Just as events in the Soviet Union had defined the limits of Eastern European politics since the war, the Gorbachev reforms were the starting point for rapid and radical changes across Eastern Europe. By the time the Soviet Communist party lost power in August 1991, Communist regimes had been swept from power across Eastern Europe.

THE REVOLUTIONS

After forty years of Soviet-dominated rule, the peoples of Eastern Europe overthrew their Communist governments in a rapid series of revolutions, beginning in 1989. Not surprisingly, given the different nature and structure of the various Eastern European countries, the revolutions took different forms and happened at different speeds. Nevertheless, once the revolutions began, the momentum was unstoppable and what had previously appeared to be the iron grip of Communist rule was swept away in one country after another.

The first countries to make the decisive move toward a Western-style system of government were the largest and the smallest: Poland and Hungary.

Poland: Solidarność triumphs

In Poland, protest against the Communist government centered on trade union activity, and grew as economic hardships worsened. As one trade unionist in the state-run Gdansk shipyard put it in 1988, "Forty years of Socialism and there's still no toilet paper." Although the demand for political reform was prominent in Poland and all the Eastern European revolutions that followed, the catalyst for change was dissatisfaction with the Communists' failure to match Western economic wealth.

In 1980, an independent trade union, Solidarność (or Solidarity), led by Lech Walesa, was established following the workers' occupation of shipyards and other industrial action. Although suppressed by martial law in the early 1980s, Solidarność was to play the leading role in the Polish revolution. In May and August 1988, strikes and workplace occupations spread across the country; the protesters' slogan was: "There's no liberty without solidarity." Meetings between the government and Solidarność had been taking place since 1987 and, at one such meeting in 1989, a deal was struck. In return for quelling the

Between 1945 and 1980, all trade unions in Communist Eastern Europe were linked with the Communist party and the state. In the 1980s, Polish opposition to Communism united around Solidarność, an independent trade union. Its leader, Lech Walesa (on the right), became Poland's president after the fall of Communism.

In the 1950s, the Hungarian leader Imre Nagy tried to introduce political and economic reforms. His efforts were rewarded by the Soviet invasion of 1956. Nagy was executed and buried outside the capital. His reburial in Budapest (shown here) in 1989 symbolized the Hungarian revolution.

strikes, the Polish government agreed to the legalization of the trade union and to hold talks with the opposition to discuss political and economic reform.

In February 1989, the two sides signed an agreement that allowed free elections for the entire upper house of the Parliament (the Senate) and 35 percent of the more important lower house (the Sejm). In the elections that followed, in June 1989, Solidarność was victorious.

After the elections, Solidarność had 99 percent of the Senate seats and 161 of 460 seats in the Sejm. Although the Communists still controlled the government, they had lost all moral authority. Wherever they had stood for election, they had been rejected by the Polish people. Communist president Jaruzelski admitted that it was "the first time that voters could choose freely. That freedom was used for the crossing off of those who were in power till now."

In Parliament, Solidarność representatives changed their name to the Citizens' Parliamentary Club (although the link between the parliamentarians and the trade union was to remain for some time) and began to push for economic reforms. It formed an alliance with the Democratic party and the United Peasants party (which had formally been "puppet" parties that always supported the Communists). As a result, the Communists were unable to form a government. The Citizens' Parliamentary Club was invited to form a government, and it did so in coalition with the two other parties in the alliance, forcing the Communists to work under their former Solidarność enemies. The Communists were eventually swept away in the first full free election in October 1991.

Hungary: reform from within

In Hungary, the first steps toward revolution were taken inside the Communist party during the 1980s, when a number of reforms were instigated by party liberals. Once the government permitted freedom of assembly and demonstrations by opposition groups in the winter of 1988-1989, these reforms were pushed along rapidly by protests and demands from the people.

On June 17, 1989, the government allowed the exhumation and proper reburial of Imre Nagy, the Hungarian leader who had been executed following the Soviet invasion of Hungary in 1956. Following his execution, he had been buried in an unmarked plot on the outskirts of the capital, Budapest.

The ceremony for Nagy attracted a crowd of

East Germans rush through a border gate from Hungary into Austria with only the possessions they can carry. Hungary's decision to open its borders to the West helped to bring about change in East Germany.

200,000 and was broadcast live on television. At the ceremony, which attracted government representatives anxious to be associated with reform as well as a wide range of opposition groups, there were demands for an end to Communist rule.

Opposition groups took part in talks with the government and in September 1989 an agreement was signed that allowed a free parliamentary election. The following month, the Communist Hungarian Socialist Workers party changed its name to the Hungarian Socialist party and a new Hungarian republic, in which Western democracy and democratic socialism were equally recognized, was proclaimed. Following free elections in March 1990, a non-Communist government took power.

East Germany: the Wall comes down
The revolution in Hungary was to be the spark that ignited the revolution of East Germany. On September 10, 1989, Hungary opened its border with Austria for the first time. Thousands of East Germans traveled to Hungary to cross the border and, much to the annoyance of the East German government, the Hungarians allowed them to cross into the West. In the first three days, 15,000 East Germans crossed into Austria; by the end of

September, 50,000 had crossed over. East Germany responded by closing its border with Czechoslovakia on October 3. Following the revolutions in Poland and Hungary and the closure of the border, Czechoslovakian opposition to East Germany's Communist leaders grew in the summer and autumn of 1989.

In October 1989, Soviet president Gorbachev visited East Germany for the 40th anniversary of the East German Communist state. He warned the government that "life itself punishes those who delay." This indicated that the Soviet Union would not interfere with political reform in East Germany as it had in other Eastern European states in the 1950s and 1960s. Opposition groups and Communist reformers were encouraged by Gorbachev's remarks.

Opposition was based in the churches where, because a large number of East Germans were churchgoers, there was considerable protection from state suppression. Every Monday evening, in the Leipzig Church of Saint Nicholas, prayers for peace were followed by small demonstrations for democratic reform. These had numbered up to 5,000 people in September and grew to more than 15,000 by October. These regular protests became the focus of the mass demonstrations against the Communist regime.

A few days after Gorbachev's visit, and following the violent repression of opposition groups during the anniversary celebrations, 70,000 people turned up to the protest in Leipzig. This time the government chose not to use force. The protests soon grew to 300,000, then half a million people.

In response to the opposition demands, the government reopened the border with Czechoslovakia (thus allowing migration to the West) and, on November 9, the Berlin Wall was opened from the East. Amid jubilant celebrations in Berlin by millions of East and West Germans over Christmas and New Year, the call for the reunification of Germany became unstoppable.

Czechoslovakia: the velvet revolution

It has been said that in Poland the revolution took ten years, in Hungary ten months, in Germany ten weeks, and in Czechoslovakia ten days. This is an exaggeration; in fact, the Czech revolution took just over a month!

It started on November 17, 1989, with a large demonstration in Prague. The protest was ended by the police, who brutally attacked the demonstrators. The following day, Prague students went on strike. They were joined by

actors on the 19th, and opposition groups then met together in the Magic Lantern Theatre in the center of Prague to form themselves into the Civic Forum and set out demands for democratic reforms.

On November 20, the students protesting in the city's massive Saint Wenceslas Square were joined by thousands of demonstrators from all walks of life. The crowds were addressed by the playwright Vaclav Havel, who had emerged as the main spokesperson of Civic Forum. On November 24, he was joined in Wenceslas Square by Alexander Dubcek, the reformist Communist leader who had been deposed following the Soviet invasion of Czechoslovakia in 1968.

On the 25th, half a million people demonstrated in the snow near the Letna football stadium, and the following day a government delegation met with Civic Forum. The government promised to release political prisoners and Prime Minister Adamec addressed the crowds, who booed and jeered him.

The Forum had called a nationwide general strike for Monday, November 27. At noon, even the Czech television reporter announced to viewers that he was leaving the TV studio to join the strike. Thousands of workers in Prague, Brno,

In November 1989, a huge crowd in Prague hails Alexander Dubcek, the ex-president of Czechoslovakia, who was deposed by the Soviet Union after the invasion of 1968. Although a lifelong Communist, Dubcek introduced political reforms in what came to be known as the "Prague Spring" of 1968.

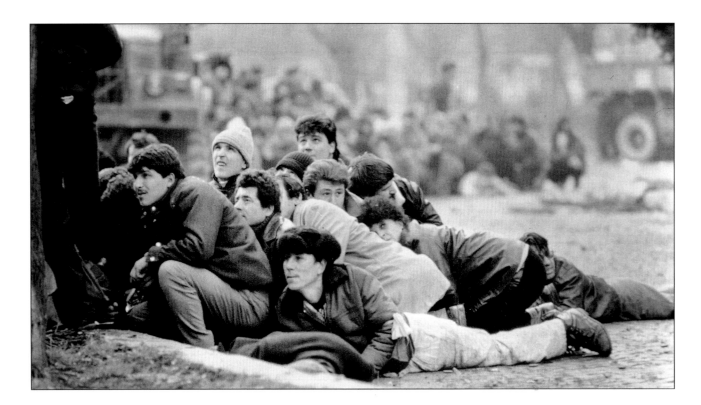

Bratislava, Ostrava, and all the major towns and cities of the country did likewise.

In the light of the protests, the government began to give in to the Forum's demands. Each time they did, more demands were made. On December 3, Prime Minister Adamec announced a new government but, as it was still to be dominated by Communists, Civic Forum threatened another general strike and more demonstrations.

As Wenceslas Square echoed to the chants of "Long live the students," "Long live the actors," and "Long live the Forum," the five Warsaw Pact states that had invaded Czechoslovakia in 1968 formally renounced and condemned the invasion. Adamec resigned on December 7 and three days later President Gustav Husak swore in a new government that consisted almost entirely of people recommended by Civic Forum. He then resigned.

Jan Carnogursky, who had been in jail two weeks before, was now a first vice premier of Czechoslovakia, with partial responsibility for the police and security apparatus. The free-market economist Vaclav Klaus became the finance minister. On December 28, Alexander

Romanians crouch to avoid Communist snipers' bullets in December 1989.

Dubcek was made chair of the Federal Assembly (the Czechoslovakian Parliament) and the next day the assembly elected Vaclav Havel as president.

By this time, the Romanian dictator Ceauşescu had been deposed and executed and the remaining Eastern European countries—Yugoslavia, Bulgaria, and Albania—were undergoing their own revolutions or were soon to do so.

Romania: death of a dictator

Under Communist president Nicolae Ceauşescu, Romania had been the harshest and most totalitarian country in Eastern Europe. The Romanian revolution was the only Eastern European revolution in which there was a great deal of violence.

As in Czechoslovakia, the revolution was very rapid. It began in December 1989 when the government announced that it was to punish Laszlo Tokes, a Hungarian pastor in the city of Timisoara, for preaching against the authorities.

When they tried to evict him to a smaller parish, his congregation formed a human chain around his home to prevent his removal.

On the following day, the people of Timisoara began a mass protest against the Communist authorities, which soon turned to rioting.

Nicolae and Elena Ceauşescu after their capture. They were tried by a military tribunal and executed on Christmas Day 1989.

President Ceauşescu ordered his troops to shoot the demonstrators but many were unwilling to do so. When Constantin Dascalescu, a leading Communist, tried to address the demonstrators, he was jeered and silenced by shouts of "Down with Ceauşescu." Soon, however, the demonstration turned to tragedy when the secret police— the Securitate—began to shoot the demonstrators. Between December 17 and 20, some 70 people were killed in the city.

On December 21, President Ceauşescu organized a rally of support in the Romanian capital, Bucharest. However, the gathering turned swiftly into a demonstration against Ceauşescu himself as people taunted him with cries of "Timisoara." The following day, the president attempted to escape the fury of his people. Many of the troops in the army had joined the demonstrators, and Ceauşescu and his wife, Elena, (who was also a high-ranking politician) were forced to flee by helicopter.

The demonstrations continued in cities across the country, but they turned into bloody battles as the Securitate continued to shoot and torture demonstrators. It is estimated that as many as 1,000 people were killed throughout the country. In Bucharest, the army took control of the television center. When the Securitate attempted to seize the building, the army appealed to the people and 3,000 demonstrators came to their aid. The Securitate withdrew, but the killings continued.

The police soon tracked down the Ceauşescus and on Christmas Day they were brought before a military tribunal and charged with genocide and "subversion of the national economy." After a summary four-hour trial, they were sentenced to death and were shot the same day.

The National Salvation Front (NSF), which itself was led by leading ex-Communists, formed a provisional government and elections were held in May 1990. The NSF won and their leader, Ion Iliescu, became president.

The revolutions had fed on hopes for more political freedoms and for a better life than Soviet-led Communism had delivered. The attempts to achieve these goals were to bring new conflicts.

THE ECONOMY

The inefficiency of the postwar Eastern European economies had meant that, by the time the revolutions began in around 1989, living standards in Eastern Europe were much lower than those in the West. These poor economic conditions were among the chief causes of the revolutions in Eastern Europe.

In economic terms, Communist countries have two distinctive features. First, the state or other institutions, such as the Communist party, own or control most of the important parts of the economy, including natural resources, industry, and transportation.

Second, while capitalist countries rely on markets and prices to exchange goods and services, Communist countries do this through central planning. The government decides what goods and services need to be produced. It allocates raw materials and capital goods to factories and farms, which are then expected to produce a certain amount of food, goods, or services. These, in turn, are distributed to shops in the cities and towns, again through central planning.

Following the revolutions, almost all of the Eastern European countries wanted to move to a Western-style economy as rapidly as possible. But this transition, which was intended to raise standards of living to Western levels, was to be very difficult. Most of the people had high expectations but others could see the difficulties ahead. At the end of Communist rule, one Hungarian said, "I'm happy to have lived to see the end of this disaster, but I want to die before the beginning of the next one." The policies necessary to make the transformation were to create new economic hardships for Eastern Europeans and lead to new conflicts.

During the years of Communist rule, the economies of Eastern Europe stagnated. This picture of a Polish farm in the 1980s could just as easily have been taken 50 years earlier.

This table shows the number of luxury items owned per 1,000 of population in Eastern European countries. Figures are also included for the USSR and the UK. All figures are for 1987, except telephones, which are 1984/1985 figures.

Country	Telephones	Radios	TVs	Cars
Albania	n/a	167	83	1.6
Bulgaria	200	221	189	115
Czechoslovakia	226	256	285	171
East Germany	212	663	754	199
Hungary	134	586	402	135
Poland	105	289	263	98
Romania	67	288	173	11
Yugoslavia	132	235	209	125
USSR	98	685	310	40
UK	523	1,145	434	292

(Source: *UNESCO Statistical Yearbook 1989*)

Most Eastern European industry was old-fashioned, inefficient, and dirty. This picture shows pollution pouring from the chimneys of a Romanian factory.

At the end of the 1980s, all of the economies of Eastern Europe were almost entirely dependent on government-owned (or "public sector") industries for employment and income. The government was responsible for the distribution of goods. What's more, consumers had little or no choice in what to buy as there was normally only one type of any product available. (This is quite unlike the situation in the West, where there is often a wide range of competing products from which shoppers can choose. For example, when you are next in a supermarket, look at the laundry detergents; there may be dozens of different brands on the shelves even though they all have the same function.) Because of these factors, there was little incentive to make sure that Eastern European goods were produced efficiently or to a high standard of quality; the manufacturers knew that people would buy their products because they had no choice.

The Eastern European nations were largely isolated from the world economy. Most exports went to the Soviet Union or other Eastern European countries under the COMECON system. For example, before 1989 Bulgaria sold 80 percent of its exports to Eastern bloc countries. Furthermore, in order to maintain its influence over Eastern Europe, the Soviet Union subsidized many of the raw materials and much of the energy used by Eastern European industry by selling them very cheap.

These factors allowed industry to become very inefficient compared to that in the West. When Communism was rejected, all the countries of Eastern Europe were forced to enter the world economy. In order to be able to buy the goods that Eastern Europeans wanted from the West, their industries had to be able to make goods that could be sold back to Western countries (see box on world trade on page 18). This meant that they had to become as efficient as Western industries, but catching up was a massive task.

Computers in use in Eastern Europe. All Western goods have to be paid for in hard currencies, which are very expensive for Eastern Europeans to obtain because their own currencies are relatively weak.

First of all, in order to improve their industrial efficiency, all the Eastern Europeans wanted to "privatize" their industries—that is, to take them out of the public sector and sell them to individuals or private companies. They hoped that by doing this they would attract investment into their economies. They also hoped that, through privatization, their economies would become more efficient as the new owners sought to increase sales and profits.

However, there were few individuals in Eastern Europe with enough wealth to buy the public sector industries. Furthermore, as the industries were so inefficient compared with those in the West, foreign companies were not prepared to pay high prices. So many of the most attractive Eastern European companies were sold at relatively low prices. This meant that selling off state-run industries brought in very little cash.

Without the protection of the Soviet Union, Eastern European countries had to import goods from the West at market prices. For Hungary, the loss of cheap Soviet oil imports cost an extra $1 billion in the first year alone.

As a result, the Eastern European governments

World trade

Suppose an Eastern European country (say, Poland) wants to buy a computer from a Western country (say, the United States). The U.S. manufacturer wants to sell its product for dollars, because it needs dollars to buy goods and services in its own country. Poland has its own currency, the zloty, and it has to exchange this for dollars in order to buy the computer.

The computers are high quality and high technology, so lots of people want to buy them. People also want to buy a whole range of American goods. This means that they all need dollars, and so dollars themselves have a fairly stable value and are widely used in world trade, between all countries. This makes them a "hard currency." (You may have noticed that this book values everything in U.S. dollars—exactly because, as a hard currency, the dollar has an internationally recognized value.)

But Polish goods are of relatively low quality and not many people want to buy them. So, although they may be cheap in Poland, they are difficult to sell abroad. Therefore, few people want zlotys with which to buy Polish goods. The zloty is, therefore, a weak currency—it is not worth much compared to the dollar.

So, for Poland, an American-made computer is very expensive because dollars are very expensive. Until Poland can improve the world demand for its goods, and so increase the value of the zloty, it has a stark choice: either go without the computer, or increase the debt it owes to richer countries.

soon found they were running up huge debts because they did not have enough money to buy the goods their people and industries needed. The more they imported Western goods to improve the quality of their own industrial output, the faster their debts rose. Yet, because the old system had collapsed, it was necessary to continue to import raw materials, components, and energy to keep industry running in order to earn hard currency to buy more goods from abroad.

To varying extents, all the Eastern European governments ran up debts. In Poland, external debt in mid-1991 stood at $30 billion even after Western countries had written off $20 billion of debt. (In other countries, such as Hungary, which had relatively stronger economies, the debt was lower.) With debts on this scale, and with the West warning that Eastern Europe could not

spend more than it earned, there was little scope to ease the transition to capitalism.

Meanwhile, industries were producing less and less. The United Nations (UN) estimated that wealth in Eastern Europe fell by 25 percent between 1988 and 1992. Industrial output in Poland dropped by 40 percent between 1990 and 1992, reducing the country's national wealth by 20 percent.

Output was falling while goods were having to be paid for with hard currency. To make matters worse, all the Eastern European countries had to lift the controls on prices that had been the norm under Communism. When subsidies on essential goods such as food and fuel were lifted, prices rose rapidly. In 1991, inflation ranged from 39 percent in Hungary to as high as 250 percent in Bulgaria and 400 percent in Romania.

The Great Boulevard in Budapest, Hungary. Central Europeans hope that tourism will grow following the collapse of Communism.

As if that were not enough, Eastern Europeans also began to experience for the first time unemployment on a large scale. One of the benefits of the Communist system was that everyone had a job, no matter how inefficient that made industry as a whole. When companies were privatized and public sector industries struggled to reduce costs, jobs were cut. In 1991, unemployment reached more than 300,000 in Hungary, more than two million in Poland, and more than three million (nearly 20 percent of the working population) in East Germany.

Their economies weakened by years of inefficiency, and their peoples burdened with unemployment and inflation, the Eastern European governments looked to the West for help. The stronger economies, such as Hungary, found it relatively easy to attract Western investment, but for others the West offered little but advice to keep on taking the harsh medicine of the free market.

After the euphoria of the revolutions, the new system came as a great shock to many Eastern Europeans. Even by mid-1992, some countries, such as Bulgaria, Romania, and Albania, still seemed far away from achieving the goal of

A plastics factory in Albania in 1991. For a time, following the end of Communist rule, economic activity ground to a halt in Albania.

Romanians, who were denied Western fashions for decades, struggle to get into their country's first Levi's jeans shop in 1991.

Western help for Eastern European economies

Western governments want to help the Eastern European countries move to a capitalist system for a number of reasons. One is political: They want capitalism to win over Communism. Another is economic: They see investment opportunities for Western firms and future opportunities to sell goods to Eastern Europe. To realize these opportunities, they need to increase wealth in Eastern European countries to enable them to afford Western goods.

A number of Western companies have already started to invest, especially in the stronger Eastern European economies. In the first nine months of 1990 alone, Hungary received some $800 million of foreign investment, mainly from large companies in the United States, Japan, and Western Europe. In 1991, it received another $1 billion.

In 1991, the European Community set up the European Bank for Reconstruction and Development, which is based in London. The aim of the bank is to give aid and help the restructuring of the Eastern European and Soviet economies, and to stimulate trade between the East and West.

However, foreign investment in Eastern Europe and the Soviet Union has been slow and its distribution has been very uneven. By October 1991, only $13 billion had been invested and most of this had gone to one country—Hungary. After the initial promise, it remains to be seen whether enough Westerners have the confidence to invest in Eastern Europe.

building efficient, competitive economies. Those with relatively "stronger" economies— Czechoslovakia, Poland, East Germany, and especially Hungary—lagged a long way behind those in the West.

The empty shops, which were common under Communism, had filled up with goods in most (though not all) of the Eastern European countries. However, wealth had fallen and fewer people could afford the goods that were available. In Czechoslovakia, spending power decreased by nearly a quarter in the first half of 1991 alone. The UN predicted that falling spending power in the region could lead to increasing social and political unrest that might threaten the stability of the whole of Europe.

GOING PRIVATE: DAILY LIFE IN EASTERN EUROPE

The revolutions of 1989 brought to an end more than forty years of stagnation and political repression. With the economic reforms that followed, daily life in Eastern Europe has been changed unimaginably.

Of course, the experiences of ordinary people vary enormously from one country to another, depending on each country's wealth and the policies it adopted after Communism. For most people, the main issue was the impact of economic reforms. For others, like those families caught up in the horrific civil wars in Yugoslavia, economic questions had relatively little immediate impact on daily life. Their experience is discussed in chapter 10.

Although it is accepted generally that economic reforms are essential, they have made day-to-day

Budapest: Private traders offer increased choice but often at prices too high for most people.

Privatization

There were basically two types of enterprise to be privatized. First were the large industrial companies. As we have seen, these were, for the most part, highly inefficient and unattractive to the Western companies—the only ones that could afford them.

However, others were extremely attractive to Western companies. In 1991 and 1992, brewing companies around the world were lining up to buy the world-famous Pilsner-Urquell brewery in Czechoslovakia. Although it would have been easy to sell at a good price, the sale became a controversial issue. Foreign investment was attractive, but many Eastern Europeans were unhappy about the prospect of selling their few efficient and profitable companies to the West.

In 1992, the government forbade the sale of Pilsner-Urquell and other leading companies to the West. Instead, it tried to sell either to Czechoslovakian banks and financial institutions or to use its "voucher" system to privatize while keeping industry in Czechoslovakian ownership.

Under the voucher system, which was expected to account for the privatization of about 40 percent of industry, citizens were entitled to a certain number of vouchers, which could be exchanged in the future for a share in public companies. However, the system was exploited by some who realized that vouchers worth $34 might be worth over $27,000 when exchanged for shares. These speculators tried to get hold of as many vouchers as possible, often by illegal means. Many ordinary citizens, who did not realize the potential worth of the vouchers, were conned.

The other type of enterprises being privatized were shops and small businesses. In Czechoslovakia, these were mainly sold at auction. Again, only a few citizens were able to participate in the privatization. Shops in the capital, Prague, were being sold for thousands of dollars—way beyond the means of all but a few Czechs.

An advertisement for Pilsner-Urquell beer. Such signs are a bitter reminder to many Czechs of the way in which they were tricked when the brewery was privatized in 1992.

life extremely hard for most ordinary Eastern Europeans. In 1991, it was estimated that while 10 percent of Hungary's population was getting richer under the reforms, most were merely holding their own and up to a third were getting poorer. There is much optimism and enthusiasm for political and economic reform in official circles, but it is seldom matched among ordinary people. An opinion poll published by the European Community in January 1992 showed that most Eastern Europeans were dissatisfied with their lack of democratic rights and their poor living standards. Many simply wanted to move to the West.

The Solidarność trade union, which began the whole process of reform in Poland, reverted to its original role as a trade union soon after the Communists were swept from power. It wanted

For most Eastern Europeans, the hardship of daily life has not gone away since the revolutions. This picture shows the interior of a an apartment in Bucharest, Romania, in 1989.

change from the old Communist system but the rapid program of change adopted by the new government saw ordinary working people bearing the brunt of the economic reforms. In January 1992, as factories closed and prices and unemployment soared because of the economic reforms, Solidarność was again calling strikes, to protest against rising prices. The response of its former allies, who were now in government, was to blame others while pressing ahead with the policies they deemed necessary to enable Poland to join the world economic community.

Unemployment hit older workers especially hard as their new employers considered them to be set in their ways and much harder to train in new working methods than younger workers. Disillusionment with the reforms grew. Privatization itself added to the disillusionment. Under Communism, the state system had at least provided work and low, stable prices for everyone. Now those in work did not know how long their jobs would last, and prices rose daily. The old certainties were gone, but the fruits of privatization appeared to be going either to foreign companies or to a few rich individuals whose wealth had been amassed by questionable means (see box on privatization on page 23).

Tax in Poland
Market economics was an entirely new experience for the countries of Eastern Europe, and it took some getting used to. Taxation, essential to government finance, caused great problems in Poland.

In 1991, tax rates were 25 percent for individuals and 40 percent for corporations. But there were only 1,500 tax inspectors for a population of 39 million. The tax inspectors had little experience and no computer support. Only slightly more than $3 million was collected in tax—in a country where the budget deficit was $1.5 billion in the first three months of 1992!

Before the revolution, 80 percent of government revenue had come from state-owned enterprises. Now that these were either in massive debt or being sold to the private sector, economic activity was moving to the private sector. However, many people in the private sector, especially those with roots in the black market, tended to avoid paying taxes. As a result, government income fell sharply.

The government hoped to improve the situation with a mixture of advice from the United States Internal Revenue Service and by offering cash rewards for informers—a strangely prerevolutionary approach!

With privatization, a small group of "entre-preneurs"were able to make a lot of money. Many of these people had been black mar-keteers before the revolutions. Others were ex-Communists or corrupt government officials who had used their positions to benefit from the new conditions.

A growing gap between rich and poor devel-oped, as did a gap between the cities and the countryside. Crime rates rose across the region, with the rule of law collapsing completely in Albania (see box on Albania). Along with the strikes and protests, political intolerance grew in response to the difficulties of daily life.

Albania: the rule of law

Nowhere in Eastern Europe was the effect of economic reform to hit harder than in Albania. Soon after the Communists lost power, the economy collapsed. Farm output fell by 50 percent in many places as people refused to work the land until it was redistributed. Industrial production fell to less than 15 percent of its previous level. By September 1991, the shops were completely empty. In 1992, the international aid agency Oxfam estimated that it would be at least two years before Albania was in a position either to grow its own food or buy food from abroad.

Aid from other European countries was interrupted by a complete collapse in the rule of law by the end of 1991. In December 1991, more than 30 people died in food riots when a depot in the northeastern town of Fushe-Arrez was burned down by looters. In the same month, two people were killed when a mob rampaged in Lac, 25 miles north of the capital, Tirana, when bread trucks failed to appear.

By 1992, looting and theft of emergency supplies by organized gangs was widespread. The cities were controlled by mob rule, with knife and gun attacks common. Water and electricity supplies were constantly interrupted and people, especially women, were frightened to leave their homes. As one Albanian woman put it, "Now we've got total freedom, but it's total chaos and we can do nothing."

The picture below shows Albanian women in the fields near Tirana.

CHAPTER 6

SELLING TO THE WORLD?

The new governments of Eastern Europe hoped that privatization would enable them to compete in world trade. However, it soon became clear that privatization on its own was not enough. Although it brought about a change of ownership, other reforms were necessary to improve Eastern Europe's manufacturing performance—and this could not be done painlessly.

Between 1990 and 1992, Poland boasted that its private sector had grown from 9 percent to 20 percent of the economy. However, this had barely affected manufacturing industries; 87 percent of new businesses were trading companies that did not actually produce anything.

Throughout Eastern Europe, the private trading and distribution sectors grew, but manufacturing was still dominated by inefficient and debt-ridden state-owned companies. It became obvious that, no matter how ambitious the privatization targets, something had to be done to make manufacturing industry work better.

One way to do this was to encourage takeovers or partnerships with successful Western firms. In Czechoslovakia, the Skoda car firm, based in the town of Mlada Boleslav, northeast of Prague, was partly taken over by the German Volkswagen company in 1990.

Skoda dominated the town. It was the biggest and most modern car company in Eastern Europe and everyone depended on it for employment— and for providing schools and shops and even funding the local football team. Now its fate was in the hands of Volkswagen, which planned to have a 70 percent stake in the company by 1994. Volkswagen planned to invest a lot of money in the factory, but it also wanted to make substantial changes in order to improve its efficiency. First of all, it said that Skoda's way of manufacturing all parts of the car on the same site was inefficient. In the future, important parts were to be made

The Skoda car factory at Mlada Boleslav, Czechoslovakia, was state-run until 1990. The German company Volkswagen aims to own 70 percent of Skoda by 1994.

Walbrzych, Poland
In spring 1991, it was announced that the coal mines of Walbrzych were to be closed because they were old-fashioned and uneconomical. In fact, they were due to be closed before World War II but were kept open for the war effort and never closed afterward because so many jobs depended on them. Although more than 233,000 people, one-sixth of the city's population, would become unemployed, there was no place for such job creation under the new market system. There were no other manufacturing jobs in the area and, because of housing shortages, it was not possible to move the people to seek work in other parts of the Upper Silesia region.

Without investment in new manufacturing or new housing, the region faced a grim future of unemployment in an area where the environment has been destroyed by pollution from the coal and coking industries.

elsewhere, including overseas. Also, the management structure and ways of working were to be changed.

Together with the fall in demand for cars in Eastern Europe, these measures led to many jobs being lost and many remaining workers working fewer hours for less money. Although the Czechs could be confident that Volkswagen would improve the market performance of the company, some workers began to wonder if the rule of the German corporation might have as many disadvantages as the Soviet dominance of the past.

On the other side of the country, the Slovakian town of Martin was experiencing different problems. Like Mlada Boleslav, Martin was a one-industry town. It was dominated by a tank factory. During the cold war, the factory had made tanks for the Czech army and, like other Czechoslovakian arms companies, had exported its products to the Warsaw Pact and other countries. Now it was hit by recession. When

Civic Forum came to power, it wanted to reduce Czechoslovakia's arms exports. But towns like Martin depended on arms exports for jobs. Arms production was concentrated in Slovakia, where unemployment was three times the national average.

In 1991, President Havel reluctantly allowed the sale of 250 T-72 tanks to Syria, saying that he hoped it would be the last such deal. Although they have work in the short term, the workers of Martin are worried that they will be unemployed once the tanks are completed.

It is very unlikely that a Western manufacturer would want to buy a tank factory that cannot make money now that the cold war is over. So the workers of Martin face a grim future unless new work can be attracted to the area. And, indeed, the Czechoslovakian manufacturing economy will also suffer further if formerly successful companies cannot find new markets.

EAST MEETS WEST

For those Eastern Europeans who expected a quick and easy transformation to Western life-styles, the early 1990s brought disillusionment. In the first two years following the revolutions, the costs of reform far outweighed the benefits for most Eastern Europeans and the good life seemed a long way off.

As this realization grew, many Eastern Europeans began to resent the West. Western governments and their peoples had cheered on the revolutions, even though they had offered little practical help to the opposition groups that had struggled under Communism. With Communism gone, the West seemed reluctant to make a strong commitment to economic regeneration in Eastern Europe.

In the face of a world recession, the Western countries argued that there was little scope to increase aid to Eastern Europe. To Eastern Europeans, who were subjected to a daily diet of Western advertising and who saw wealthy Western tourists enjoying their new access to the

Albanian refugees crowd the quayside at Bari, Italy, in August 1991. Over 12,000 arrived, only to be sent back to Albania.

Not all Germans were happy about the reunification of their country. On October 3, 1990—the day on which East and West Germany were reunited—these people held a demonstration in Berlin.

East, this argument was less than convincing.

Nowhere was the meeting between East and West demonstrated more starkly than in Germany. Germany had been divided into East and West as part of the postwar settlement between the Soviet Union and the United States. Partly, the division reflected the practical fact that Soviet and Western troops had met in Germany as they simultaneously converged on Hitler's forces at the end of World War II. There was also a deeper reason for the division. From the point of view of the Soviet Union, which had lost 20 million people during the Nazi invasion, the division of Germany meant that the country could no longer be an economic or military threat to its neighbors.

However, as the cold war progressed, Western countries, and especially West Germany, insisted that Germany should one day be reunited. This ideal was not shared by some of the opposition forces in East Germany, who dreamed instead of building on some of the positive aspects of the

East, such as greater equality and a stronger sense of community and solidarity, to create a new and more democratic form of socialism. Prior to and during the revolution, for example, the churches in East Germany had referred to themselves as the "Church in Socialism."

However, East Germans' fears of being sucked into the West German system were soon to become a reality. When the Berlin Wall came down, calls for German reunification became louder from West and East alike. Many East Germans wanted a share in the material wealth of West Germany, which had become Europe's strongest and most stable economy in the postwar years. West Germans wanted to realize a political dream, but they were worried about the flood of East German immigrants who were threatening to overwhelm the West German job market and social services. Despite such fears,

Chancellor Helmut Kohl of Germany. Unification had been a long-standing goal for many Germans but its reality brought many political and economic problems.

the desire for change grew and East and West Germany were reunited on October 3, 1990.

At first, the new Germany was full of optimism. Chancellor Helmut Kohl won the first general elections of the united Germany on the promise that the German "economic miracle" would continue and that within five years East Germans would enjoy the same wealth as their new compatriots in the West. However, it soon became clear that it was not possible to fulfill this promise and West Germans came to see East Germany as a burden.

Although the former West Germany invested $60 billion in what had been East Germany between 1989 and 1991, the eastern part of the country was able to contribute very little to the economic development of the new Germany. In 1991, only 7 percent of Germany's total economic growth came from the East. Meanwhile, it was estimated that reunification costs could reach 527 billion deutsch marks (about $370 billion) by the mid-1990s.

After reunification, Germany's wealth stopped growing in the way it had done in West Germany in the past—and there were now 17 million extra Germans to share the wealth. In the united Germany, debt grew to 1.8 trillion deutsch marks (about $1.26 trillion) in 1992, inflation rose to 5 percent—the highest figure for ten years—and taxes rose, too.

West Germans began to resent paying for reunification. They regarded East Germans as lazy and unproductive. In the spring of 1992, public and private sector workers in the West went on strike for higher wages, saying that they would not pay for reunification out of their own pockets.

Meanwhile, in the eastern half of the new Germany, economic conditions deteriorated quickly. Eastern Europeans were used to full employment, but now more than three million were out of work. Industries were sold at low prices to Western companies that often merely closed down large parts of them. The high rents and other costs that came with capitalism made it impossible for all but a few East Germans to benefit directly from privatization.

April 1991: German neo-Nazis greet Polish tourists with fascist salutes and chants of "Germany for the Germans."

People soon realized that reunification was not going to mean the same good life for all citizens of the new Germany. In 1992, a group of German economists said that Chancellor Kohl's aim of equality between East and West within five years was not achievable; it would be twenty years at least before people in the East enjoyed the same wealth as those in the West. If it were to be achieved at all, it would cost 1.85 trillion deutsch marks (about $1.3 trillion). Resentment in the West of the costs of reunification was matched in the East by the disappointment and bitterness at being seen as the "poor relatives." Increasingly, East Germans felt that they had not experienced reunification, but colonization by the West.

The rise of the Right in Germany
One effect of the growing economic problems in Germany has been the rise of extreme right-wing neo-Nazi groups, encouraged by the nationalist vision of German reunification. Violent neo-Nazi groups, who shared the views of Adolf Hitler (Germany's leader before and during World War II) and his followers, emerged across the country. Their targets were foreigners who had gone to Germany hoping to be allowed to live there permanently. In 1991, 256,000 would-be immigrants went to Germany, many of them from the former Communist countries of Romania and Yugoslavia.

In the autumn of 1991, there was a series of violent attacks on such refugees. In September, neo-Nazis, with the support of many local people, lay seige to a hostel for 230 asylum-seekers in Hoyerswerda in Saxony. The following month, a refugee hostel in Immenstadt, Bavaria, was burned down and neo-Nazis fought street battles with Turkish workers near Hamburg.

In the regional elections of April 1992, the German People's Union (a neo-Nazi party) gained votes in a number of regions. In Schleswig-Holstein, they got 6.3 percent of the vote, while in the Baden-Württemberg area, they won 10.9 percent of the votes and 15 of the 146 seats in the regional Parliament.

POLITICS AND DEMOCRACY

Before the revolutions of 1989, all the institutions of government and the economy in Eastern Europe were dominated by Communists who, to varying degrees, followed the Soviet model. Although not all the countries of Eastern Europe were run in exactly the same way, in every case democratic debate was stifled, and most of the revolutions were driven partly by a desire for democracy. However, building democracy proved to be much harder than defeating the Communists.

As in so many other ways, the experiences of different Eastern European countries varied enormously. East Germany, for example, became part of the "ready-made" West German state before it had an opportunity to develop its own political identity or institutions. As we saw in the previous chapter, there were both advantages and disadvantages to this.

In Romania and Bulgaria, the former Communists managed to keep a share of government. In Bulgaria, they achieved this by entering into a coalition with other groups, although they were narrowly defeated by the opposition coalition, the Union of Democratic Forces, in late 1991. In Romania, although the Communist party disappeared after the revolution, it was replaced by the National Salvation Front (NSF), made up largely of former Communists. The NSF won an outright victory in the elections of May 1990. The state of Yugoslavia collapsed quickly into civil war after the Communists were defeated, which

Although he had been a leading Communist under the Ceauşescu regime, Ion Iliescu (center) was elected president (in May 1990) following the Romanian revolution.

undermined any efforts to move toward democracy.

Many of the former Communist countries in Eastern Europe, however, shared common political experiences and problems as they worked to build a new political model.

Unity

Before democratic governments could be established, it was necessary to find out what people wanted from those who governed them. Prior to 1989, it was possible to build political unity around one simple, overriding platform—anti-Communism. Once the Communists were gone, it was vital to form political groups that could voice the different opinions and needs of the people, groups that were large and united enough to form effective governments.

In most countries, no single political party was popular enough to win an election outright. Politicians with different views and ideas were obliged to share power in coalitions. In Hungary, for example, the Hungarian Democratic Forum (MDF) governed with the support of the conservative Christian Democratic party and the Smallholders party (which represented rural interests). In Bulgaria, the Union of Democratic Forces (itself a coalition of nearly twenty political movements) ruled with the formerly Communist Socialist party, and later with a Muslim party, the Movement for Rights and Freedom.

The situation in Poland was much less clear-cut and the coalition more fragmented. First of all, there was a very low turnout in the parliamentary elections of November 1991; only 43 percent of eligible voters actually cast a vote. This reflected the people's growing disillusionment with their politicians.

When the votes were counted, no single political party won more than 13 percent of the vote and twenty-nine parties, including small groups like the Polish Beer Lovers' party, won seats in Parliament. The peculiarities of the voting system, which allowed some representatives to be elected with as few as 1,500 votes, caused some people to question the whole nature of the democracy itself. Furthermore, the confusion

Following Poland's first free elections, twenty-nine parties were represented in Parliament; none had an overall majority.

that followed made it very difficult to form an effective government with a clear direction. A delicate consensus had to be put together to carry through even the most minor decisions in Parliament.

The constitution

In Poland, the confusion allowed the president, former Solidarność leader Lech Walesa, to claim more powers for himself. This reflected a second problem that arose often in the new Eastern European democracies: How was political power to be divided among heads of state (the presidents), governments (the winning parties), and parliaments (the elected representatives)?

In Poland, Lech Walesa had enormous

Eastern European parliaments:

Hungary The Parliament is called the *orszaggyules*. From 1990, the Hungarian Democratic Forum ruled in coalition with the Christian Democrats and the Smallholders party. Of the three main opposition parties, the Free Democrats were the largest, followed by the Young Democrats and the Socialists.

Poland After elections in 1991, the lower house of the Parliament had twenty-nine parties, none with more than 13 percent of the vote. The largest party was the right-wing Catholic Democratic Union, which led a coalition.

Bulgaria Following elections immediately after the revolution, the Union of Democratic Forces ruled in coalition with the formerly Communist Socialist party. The Union of Democratic Forces (itself a coalition of nearly twenty political movements) won most seats, but not an overall majority, in the elections of autumn 1991. The Movement for Rights and Freedom held the balance of power.

East Germany Became part of a reunited Germany in 1990 and shared West Germany's existing political institutions. The West German parties now operate in all of Germany. After the German election of December 1990, the conservative Christian Democrats held power, with the minority support of the Free Democrats.

Czechoslovakia Civic Forum controlled the national government following the revolution, with the free marketeers in ascendency in the Forum. In Czechoslovakia, there have been calls to dissolve the federal republic, and this matter is currently being debated in Parliament. It is not certain whether the act for dissolution will obtain the necessary two-thirds majority in Parliament that is required for a change to the constitution, but it is likely that the breakup will go ahead anyway. When the separation happens, the Federal Assembly will cease to exist and its powers will devolve to the Czech and Slovak National Committees.

Romania The National Salvation Front, led by the ex-Communist Ion Iliescu, won elections in 1990. In 1992, the National Salvation Front split into two parties: the conservative Democratic National Salvation Front and the more reformist National Salvation Front. In elections held in September 1992, the Democratic National Salvation Front emerged as the largest single party and Ion Iliescu was reelected president.

Albania Elections held in March 1992 resulted in the opposition Democratic party (DP) obtaining 60 percent of the vote and taking control of the government. The DP is committed to a market economy and to the establishment of liberal democracy. The previous government party, the Albanian Workers party (renamed the Albanian Socialist party), had won the first free election in 1991, but had been forced to resign in December 1991 under pressure from the DP and amid worsening social disorder.

influence partly because of his charisma and partly because of the respect he gained from leading Solidarność in the 1980s. However, his tendency to claim powers for himself undermined the authority of the elected Parliament and, thus, of the democracy itself. Many Poles wondered whether a system that gave so much power to one man was truly democratic.

This question also emerged, though generally to a lesser extent, in other countries that, like Poland, elected their presidents by a direct vote of the people. Under this system, also adopted by Romania and Bulgaria, the political power of the president was very considerable. In other countries, such as Czechoslovakia and Hungary, where the president was not directly elected but simply chosen by Parliament, the president was

Lech Walesa is sworn in as Polish president in December 1990.

A Romanian woman is dragged away by miners while another miner tries to hit her with a club. In 1990, the miners, who supported Ion Iliescu's government, effectively quashed prodemocracy demonstrations.

essentially a ceremonial head of state with little direct influence on policy.

Other political forces

In countries where the president had wide influence, tensions between Parliament and president developed. These allowed other groups and institutions to use their influence, often in an undemocratic way. When it was unclear where the center of power lay, politicians—and especially presidents—tried to strengthen their position by seeking either the support or the authority of other groups. In Poland, for example, Lech Walesa courted the armed forces, who became loyal to him.

In such situations, open democracy was threatened because unelected forces were able to exert far too much influence over a powerful president in exchange for their support. Also, by courting the military and security forces, the presidents signaled that, under certain circumstances, they were prepared to use the threat of force against their populations or at least their political opponents. This was especially ironic as, on the whole, the security forces in Eastern Europe were still controlled by ex-Communists.

In Romania, too, the ex-Communist president

Ion Iliescu had the support of the security forces. In 1991, he also encouraged groups of industrial workers—mostly miners loyal to him—to put down demonstrations for democracy.

The *nomenklatura*

A common problem across Eastern Europe was that the day-to-day running of a country (as opposed to decisions over policy that were taken in its parliament) necessarily fell to the same civil servants who had previously worked for the Communist regimes. Communism had put into place massive bureaucracies that were both sympathetic to the Communists and appallingly inefficient. This powerful group, known as the *nomenklatura*, remained in the grip of Communist sympathizers in the armed forces, the security forces, and the civil service.

Initially, it was feared that Communist civil servants would attempt to stop the tide of change away from Communism. Later, fears grew that the inefficiency, corruption, and bureaucracy of the *nomenklatura* would continue to hold back democracy and economic efficiency in Eastern Europe. For example, there was evidence that senior civil servants, many of them ex-Communists, were among the few people able to buy businesses and property under privatization. This was because many had been corrupt during the Communist years and had saved large personal fortunes.

Looking back

In the early 1990s, the Eastern European countries faced the massive task of trying to build and develop democratic systems of government while also undergoing economic restructuring, legal reform, and often suffering ethnic problems. For some, the task of building a new democratic culture seemed less attractive than looking to the past—beyond Communism to the old royalist system. No Eastern European state reverted to monarchism, although there was a narrow strand of opinion that wanted to return to what it saw as a glorious past.

Dealing with the more immediate past led to further controversy. Many of the prodemocracy movements in Eastern Europe were split over what to do about ex-Communists, particularly those who were accused of repressive acts before or during the revolutions. In 1991, some in Czechoslovakia called for lists of police agents to

Where do old revolutionaries go?
In general, the revolutions of Eastern Europe were not led by politicians. In Czechoslovakia, for example, the revolution was started by students and actors but was soon bolstered by people from all walks of life.

As we saw in chapter 3, some of these people went into government. In Czechoslovakia, Civic Forum split once it was in power. A liberal faction was led by the then foreign minister, Jiri Dienstbier, while the right-wing faction, associated with the free-market economics of the then finance minister, Vaclav Klaus, gained the upper hand.

Many of the people who led the revolutions went back to their old occupations or took advantage of new opportunities. One ex-member of the Czech human rights group Charter 77 told a Western journalist in 1992, "There is a time for revolution and a time for making money. The stupid members of Charter 77 are sitting in the government. The clever ones are in business."

Hamburger bars and street beggars have appeared in postrevolution Eastern Europe.

be published and ex-Communists to be banned from office. In December of that year, it was made an offense to "promote Communism." In Hungary, it was made possible for individuals to bring charges of treason and murder against officials of the old regime. By 1992, the Hungarian government was being accused of trying to silence its critics in the media, much as the old Communist government had done.

In East Germany, lists were published of people who were informers under the Communists. The backlash against ex-Communists was a problem for a number of reasons. First of all, it was often difficult to draw the line between those who had been in control of society and those who simply colluded with the Communists to protect themselves or their careers. Second, the banning of Communism itself, while understandable, was undemocratic.

Finally, many felt that dwelling on the past and placing blame on individuals would create new divisions in societies where unity and cooperation were essential. In East Germany, civil rights groups, who had been instrumental in the revolution and who were worried about the new "atmosphere of witch-hunt and denunciation," tried to promote dialogue between the victims of Communism and its perpetrators through a group called the New Forum for Explanation and Renewal.

Scapegoats

Many Eastern Europeans have not been allowed to enjoy the new democracy. A number of minority groups have been excluded by racism and prejudice.

In Romania, the gypsy— or Rom—population was persecuted under the new regime. For centuries, the Rom, a nomadic people who originated in northern India, have been victims of racism, and half a million were gassed by the Nazis in World War II.

Although Rom formed about 10 percent of the Romanian population, after the breakup of Communism they became the victims of

A Rom family in Bucharest, Romania. Many families like this one are subject to persecution in Romania and other parts of Eastern Europe.

hatred and discrimination. This was partly because many Rom became entrepreneurs and they were made the scapegoats for all the economic difficulties that came with the transition to a free-market economy.

Many other Rom lived in abject poverty and were presented in media and intellectual circles as nothing but thieves and criminals. Increasingly, they became the victims of organized attacks by gangs. Early in 1991, more than a thousand Romanians marched on a Rom settlement in the eastern village of Mihai Kogalniceanu and burned it to the ground.

The Rom were represented in Parliament, and the Romanian president Ion Iliescu was keen to gain the support of their deputies. Yet this did not stop one Romanian independent weekly journal, *Nu* (meaning "new"), from publishing an article in 1991 with the headline, "Should we exterminate the gypsies?"

Although persecution was supposed to be a thing of the past in the new democracies of Eastern Europe, prejudice against Rom was common in other states, too. In Czechoslovakia, for example, they were widely blamed for the soaring crime rate in the cities.

PRIESTS AND POLITICS

I n November 1991, Pope John Paul II, head of the Roman Catholic church, convened the first Synod of European Bishops. The meeting, which was attended mainly by bishops from Eastern and central Europe, was to discuss the consequences for the church following the collapse of Communism in Eastern Europe and the Soviet Union.

The pope, himself a Pole, hoped for two things. First, he wanted to build up the church in Eastern Europe. Second, he wanted to use the Eastern European church as a base from which to challenge what he saw as the "secularism" and "materialism" of the West.

In Poland, the Catholic church had played an important role in opposing Communism. Nine out of ten Poles were Catholics, and the church had given leadership by preaching against Communism. It had also harbored Solidarność activists and provided money for the opposition during the difficult years of martial law. (The Protestant churches had played a similar role in the opposition in East Germany, although they were not opposed to socialism as such.)

Polish-born Pope John Paul II celebrating an open-air mass at Wroclaw, Poland, in 1983

Cardinal Glemp of Poland (center) angered many people when he spoke in favor of maintaining strong links between the state and the Catholic church.

After the Communists were defeated, the Christian influence in Poland diminished, as fewer people went to church. However, many politicians in the government were active Catholics and the church enjoyed substantial influence over Polish politics. Indeed, a government and Church Council had been established to formalize the relationship.

In 1991, the Catholic primate of Poland, Cardinal Glemp, spoke out against the separation of church and state, and resentment of the church's role in politics grew rapidly. Soon afterward, when Catholic senators tried to ban abortion, an angry debate took place. Opinion polls showed that 90 percent of Poles approved of abortion in certain circumstances and that 50 percent thought that abortion should be freely available. In the light of this, a proposed referendum on the issue was shelved.

When the Polish bishops called for voters to support candidates with "Christian values" in the October 1991 elections (they particularly supported the Christian-nationalist Catholic Electoral Action group) they lost even more public respect. Increasingly, the church became an object of ridicule. Before the revolution, Poles had insulted the "reds" (Communists); after it, they jeered the "blacks" (priests).

Nevertheless, religious issues were to continue to play a part in Eastern European politics and in some of the ethnic conflicts. In particular, the relationships between Catholics, Eastern Orthodox Christians, and Muslims were to be an important part in the conflict in Yugoslavia.

ETHNIC CONFLICT

During the Communist years following World War II, many of the ethnic conflicts that had existed for centuries in Eastern Europe were suppressed. Under Communism, ethnic and national loyalties were thought to be less important than class loyalty and solidarity between the Communist countries. As a result, many ethnic conflicts had been buried rather than resolved. Once Communism was defeated, they came to the surface in many parts of Eastern Europe but especially in Yugoslavia, which sank into civil war starting in the summer of 1991.

Yugoslavia, which means "land of the southern Slavs," was created at the end of World War I in 1918. It brought together six republics: Serbia, Croatia, Slovenia, Bosnia-Herzegovina, Montenegro, and Macedonia. Two self-governing provinces, Kossovo and Vojvodina, were created in the 1970s.

After World War II, the Communists ruled under Marshal Tito, the charismatic partisan leader who had united Yugoslavs of all ethnic groups against the Nazis. Under Tito, Yugoslavia pursued independence from the Soviet Union and became a nonaligned state. Considerable powers were given to the republics, including separate constitutions, parliaments, and elected presidents.

After Tito's death in 1980, central Yugoslav control was weakened, although a federal presidency was set up to control, among other things, foreign policy and the army. From 1989, the federal president (Ante Markovic at that

Serbian troops prepare to fire on Muslims in northern Bosnia-Herzegovina in April 1992.

Flames engulf the beautiful and historic walled city of Dubrovnik following an artillery attack by Serbian forces during the civil war in what was formerly Yugoslavia.

time) sought to liberalize the country's political institutions, abolish the Communists' monopoly of power, and encourage free-market economics. In elections the following year, nationalist presidents came to power in all six republics.

By 1990, the total population of Yugoslavia was 23.5 million, 40 percent of whom were Serbians. The population in each of the republics was made up of a mix of nationalities and ethnic groups, including Serbs, Croats, Macedonians, and Muslims, as well as smaller numbers of Hungarians, Albanians, and Turks. In addition, the country had an unusual religious mixture of Catholics and Eastern Orthodox Christians as well as the Muslims.

Once central Communist power receded, the country could not hold together. One by one, beginning with Slovenia and Croatia, the republics declared their independence from the Yugoslav Federation. This was resisted by Serbia, which was used to dominating the country and whose leaders wanted to maintain a Communist federation.

The substantial Serb minorities in the republics that intended to become independent were alarmed at being separated from Serbia, and Serbia played on and exaggerated their fears. There were 600,000 ethnic Serbs living in Croatia. When independence was declared, Serbian militia groups began to attack Croatian towns, and they were supported by the Serb-dominated federal armed forces, which annexed parts of Croatia that they said were populated mostly by Serbs.

From the summer of 1991, a bloody war was waged in Croatia in which thousands were killed (many civilians, women, and children among them) and 600,000 were driven from their homes.

POLAND
Population: 98% ethnic Polish. Apart from a small German population and a few Ukrainians and Belorussians, most ethnic minorities fled before the Second World War or were killed or moved by the Nazis.

CZECHOSLOVAKIA
Now known as the Czech and Slovak Federal Republic. Slovak nationalists want full independence. Some Moravians in central Czechoslovakia want a separate Moravian state.

HUNGARY
Poplaution: 92% ethnic Hungarian, 5% gypsy, 2% German, 1% Slovak. Hungary has very little ethnic tension.

ROMANIA
Population: 89% Romanian, 8% Hungarian, 2% German and 1% other ethnic groups. Hungarians in Transylvania say they are discriminated against by Romanians.

BERLIN ●
Warsaw ●

GERMANY
POLAND

Prague ●
THE CZECH LANDS
BOHEMIA   MORAVIA
SLOVAKIA
Bratislava ●

Budapest ●

FORMERLY YUGOSLAVIA
Slovenia Population: 95% Slovenian, 5% others. Declared independence in June 1991.

Croatia Population: 80% Croat, 12% Serb, 8% other. Declared independence in June 1991. Fighting between Croats and Serbs.

Bosnia-Herzegovina Population: 44% Muslim, 31% Serb, 17% Croat, 8% others. Declared independence in March 1992. Serbs have been fighting Muslim Bosnians for control of territory and forcing them to leave. There has been fighting between Croats and Bosnians.

Federal Republic of Yugoslavia:
Serbia Population: 66% Serb, 18% Albanian, 4% Hungarian, 3% Muslim, 9% others. Claims to be the new Yugoslav state. Contains two provinces:
1) Kosovo. 90% of population are Albanians. They claim they are discriminated against by Serbian authorities.
2) Vojvodina. Has a large Hungarian population in the north.
Montenegro Population: 95% Montenegran. Voted to stay with Serbia in a new Yugoslavia.

Macedonia Population: 67% Macedonian, 20% Albanian, 2% Serb, 11% others. Declared independence in November 1991. The Albanian minority wants to rule itself.

Ljubljana ●
SLOVENIA
Zagreb ●
CROATIA   VOJVODINA
BOSNIA-
HERZEGOVINA   Belgrade ●
FEDERAL
REPUBLIC OF
YUGOSLAVIA
Sarajevo ●   SERBIA
MONTENEGRO   KOSOVO

HUNGARY
ROMANIA
Bucharest ●

Sofia ●
BULGARIA

ALBANIA
Skopje ●
Tirana ●   MACEDONIA

BULGARIA
Population: 85% ethnic Bulgarian, 9% Turk, 3% gypsy, 2% Macedonian. There is tension between Bulgarians and Turks near the Turkish border.

ALBANIA
Population: 98% ethnic Albanian with small Greek, Macedonian, Bulgarian and gypsy minorities. The Albanian president has called for the independence of Kosovo in neighbouring Serbia.

Since the fall of Communism, conflicts have surfaced among the various ethnic groups in many Eastern European countries.

0   200   400   600   800 km

Ethnic tensions in Eastern Europe

There are a number of ethnic and territorial problems across Eastern Europe, although none is nearly as serious as those that have torn apart Yugoslavia.

Tensions between Romanians and the ethnic Hungarians who live in the west of the country have erupted into fighting on occasion and have cooled relations between Hungary and Romania. Some groups in Romania also claim that the former Soviet state of Moldova rightly belongs to Romania. Russian-speaking Moldovan Communists have formed a breakaway "Dnestr Soviet Socialist Republic" on the grounds that they fear they would become second-class citizens if united with Romania, as many ethnic Moldovans want.

In Poland and Romania, Jews have been the victims of discrimination. Although most Eastern European Jews were murdered by the Nazis during World War II, those who remain have once again become scapegoats for economic problems.

There are also up to three million ethnic Germans living in other parts of Eastern Europe, notably Poland and the north of Czechoslovakia. Shortly after reunification, Germany hinted that it had territorial rights to the part of Poland where most of the ethnic Germans lived, but such ideas were quickly shelved because they were so controversial (in that they echoed claims made by Adolf Hitler before World War II).

However, many ethnic Germans living in Poland would like to be a part of Germany.

The two separate republics of Czech and Slovakia (which make up Czechoslovakia) are still attempting to define the relationship between the separate republics and the union. Even under the Communists, there were two separate republics and, although few Slovaks want independence, there are calls for greater autonomy. Ethnic tension is mounting in Slovakia and the Slovak government of Vladimir Meciar is exploiting national rivalries. Many Czechs have already left Slovakia. Members of the Slovak government have also made strong verbal attacks on Slovakia's large Gypsy and Hungarian minorities.

European Community peace negotiator Lord Carrington (left) during talks aimed at ending the fighting in former Yugoslavia

As nationalist groups grew in strength and numbers on both sides, fueled by rumors of atrocities, the war intensified. Towns and villages across the republic were destroyed or severely damaged, including the historic port of Dubrovnik and the town of Vukovar.

International institutions like the European Community (EC) and the United Nations (UN) tried in vain to stop the fighting by negotiation and, eventually, with economic sanctions against Serbia. By the time they reached an agreement, Serbia had occupied between a quarter and a third of Croatian territory.

Early in 1992, as the international community recognized the independence of Slovenia, Croatia, and Bosnia-Herzegovina, the Serbians began a similar attack on Bosnia-Herzegovina. Of its 4.3 million inhabitants, 44 percent were Muslim, 33 percent Serb and 17 percent Croatian.

As the capital, Sarajevo, came under Serbian attack, another bloody war ensued, pitching former neighbors and friends against one another for little obvious cause apart from the territorial ambition of Serbia. As the fighting intensified and the death toll rose, it was difficult to see how Yugoslavia's many ethnic and religious groups, who had formally lived together in peace, could again be reconciled. Until there is lasting peace, political and economic development in the Yugoslav republics is impossible.

CHAPTER 11

THE NEW EASTERN EUROPE IN THE WORLD

In the three years between 1989 and 1992, Eastern Europeans experienced the most far-reaching changes imaginable. By mid-1992, many of the problems that had emerged were far from being resolved. In particular, the future role of Eastern Europe in the world was still extremely uncertain. For many Eastern Europeans, the end of Soviet influence presented an opportunity both to rebuild their historical relationships with other countries and to forge a new identity as equals with the Western nations. In particular, the central European nations of Czechoslovakia, Hungary, and Poland hoped to rejoin the mainstream of European politics and economics by joining the European Community.

By 1992, East Germany had been reunited with West Germany. Hungary, Poland, and

The European Community headquarters in Brussels, Belgium. Most Eastern European countries hope to become members of the EC as soon as possible.

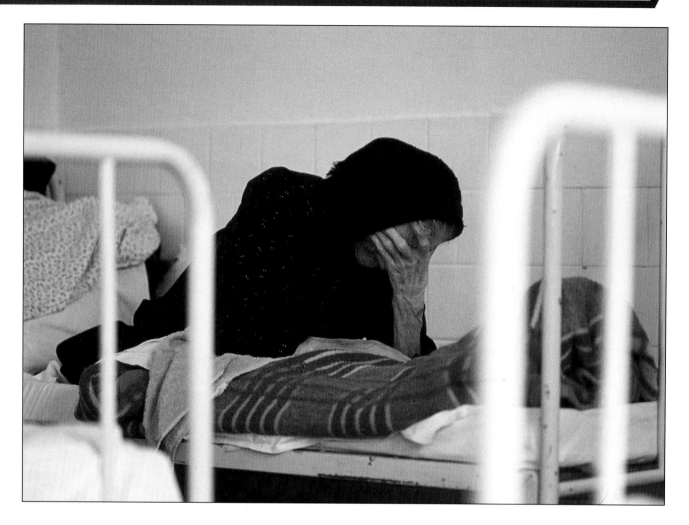

The conflict in what was Yugoslavia has left thousands of people dead and has caused many more to flee their homes. This picture shows refugees who have fled to Hungary.

Czechoslovakia looked forward to the day when their new associate membership of the European Community could become full and formal membership. Yet, in the meantime, the suspicion persisted that the Westerners who had cheered the revolutions now saw Eastern Europe as, at worst, a burden and, at best, a chance to make easy money against the background of world recession. Easterners questioned whether the West was interested in genuine cooperation on equal terms or mere exploitation.

For other Eastern Europeans—in Bulgaria, Romania, Yugoslavia, and Albania—there seemed to be little hope of sharing in the economic, political, and cultural developments enjoyed by other Europeans. Indeed, in Yugoslavia, the institutions of world order, including the European Community and the United Nations, were unable to protect ordinary people against the violent acts of nationalists.

Furthermore, with Soviet control consigned to history, Eastern Europeans were disappointed to find that global financial institutions (such as the World Bank and the International Monetary Fund) could assert their own influence over Eastern European policy in exchange for economic assistance.

Many Eastern Europeans are still hopeful. Even if times are hard and new conflicts have arisen, almost anything seems preferable to the economic and political stagnation of the years of Soviet dominance. Yet further challenges and conflicts almost certainly lie ahead for the long-suffering peoples of Eastern Europe.

GLOSSARY

Atheistic   Not believing in any god.

Black market   A system in which goods are bought and sold illegally, usually to avoid taxes, rationing, or other state controls.

Capitalism   A political and economic system in which most property is owned by individuals or private companies and not by the state. Goods compete with each other for sale in a free market and their prices are not subsidized by governments.

Catholic church   A worldwide Christian church led by the pope.

COMECON   (Council for Mutual Economic Assistance, or CMEA) COMECON was set up by the USSR in January 1949 to assist the economic development and integration of the Soviet bloc. Its full members included the USSR, Bulgaria, Czechoslovakia, East Germany, Hungary, Poland, Romania, Mongolia, Cuba, and Vietnam. COMECON was abolished in June 1991.

Command economy   An economy in which all economic decisions are taken by the state (a process known as central planning). For example, the state decides how much of a certain commodity should be produced, how and where it will be sold, and at what price. Most command economies are in Communist countries. Compare with *Market economy*.

Communism   A political and economic system in which all property is owned by the community as a whole and not by private citizens or companies. In practice, the state owns the means of production (factories, farms, and so on) and distribution (transportation, shops, etc.), and the economy is controlled by central planning. In many Communist countries, all housing is also state-owned.

Components   The individual parts that go to make up a product. For example, a microchip is a component of a computer.

Deposed   Removed from a position of power (usually political).

Eastern bloc   A name given to the group of Eastern European countries and the Soviet Union.

Economic output   The goods and services produced by an economy.

Ethnic   Relating to racial groups or characteristics.

European Community (EC)   An organization of European countries through which members agree on common economic and social policies.

Currently there are 12 member states: Belgium, Denmark, France, Germany, Greece, Ireland, Italy, Luxembourg, the Netherlands, Portugal, Spain, and the UK; several other countries have applied to join.

GDP   Short for gross domestic product; a measure of the wealth of a country.

Hard currency   A strong, stable currency that is acceptable to everyone in international trade. Dollars, deutsch marks, yen, and sterling are hard currencies.

Ideology   A set of beliefs.

Industrial action   When workers (usually in trade unions) disrupt production by going on strike, for example.

Inflation   A situation in which the prices of goods and services rise. When there is inflation, the real value of money falls because each dollar is able to buy less than it did previously.

International Monetary Fund (IMF)   A financial agency formed in 1945 to help expand world trade and give financial assistance to countries in need.

Market economy   An economy based on the principles of capitalism (*see* above). The prices of goods and services, people's wages, and what goods are made and sold are all decided by the market forces of supply (how much of a certain commodity is available) and demand (how many people want to buy it). Goods and services are sold for more than the cost of producing them in order to make profits for the companies that make and sell them. In true market economies, there is no interference (such as the payment of subsidies) by governments but, in practice, most Western economies are a mix of market economic principles and some state control. Compare with *Command economy*.

Market prices   The prices at which products sell without government subsidies.

Martial law   The imposition of military rule on the civilian population of a country.

Monarchism   System of government in which a monarch (a king or queen) holds power.

Muslim   A person who follows the Islamic religion.

Neo-Nazi   A member of a political group with an ideology similar to that of Adolf Hitler's Nazi party, which came to power in Germany in 1933. Nazism combined a fanatical sense of nationalism and belief in racial supremacy with the suppression of democracy and the persecution or extermination of political opponents and certain ethnic groups, such as the Jews and Rom, whom Nazis regarded as being racially inferior.

nomenklatura   Communist bureaucracy.

Nonaligned   A country that does not belong to a formal military or political pact. During the cold war, there was a group of nonaligned countries in the UN.

Orthodox Church   (Sometimes called the Eastern Orthodox Church)   A Christian religion of the Soviet Union and Eastern Europe.

Output   *see Economic output*

Privatize   To transfer a state-owned business or property to private ownership.

Public sector   The part of an economy that is owned and run by the state.

Recession   An economic situation in which the demand for goods and services is low, economic output is level or falling, and unemployment is rising. An economy is usually said to be in recession when the GDP (*see* above) falls for two successive three-month periods.

Rom   A nomadic ethnic group originally from northern India, now found in Eastern Europe. They are sometimes called Gypsies, although Rom usually reject this title.

Secular   Not religious.

Solidarność   A Polish trade union. *Solidarność* means "solidarity."

Subsidize   To give financial help, or "subsidy." The word is normally used to describe financial aid given by governments to industries.

United Nations (UN)   An international organization that aims to maintain peace and agreement among nations. Almost all countries are members.

Warsaw Pact   The countries that signed the East European Mutual Assistance Treaty in Warsaw, Poland, in 1955. These were Albania (which withdrew in 1968), Bulgaria, Czechoslovakia, East Germany, Hungary, Poland, Romania, and the Soviet Union. The pact established a unified military command for the countries' armed forces.

World Bank   Another name for the International Bank for Reconstruction and Development, which was formed in 1945 to help raise standards of living in developing countries.

FURTHER INFORMATION

For a more detailed look at the events of 1989 and after, read copies of newspapers. The best way to do this is to go to your local reference library, where newspapers are kept on microfilm. You can find key articles that are worth reading by looking at the headlines. Magazines such as *Time, Newsweek,* and *U.S. News & World Report* also regularly cover events in eastern Europe.

Television news shows are excellent sources of up-to-the-minute information. You can find out what is currently happening in Eastern Europe and all around the world by watching the nightly news and shows such as *Nightline* and *60 Minutes.* Many stations also present special news shows to cover very important events.

Books on the history of Eastern Europe up to 1989

Brogan, Patrick. *The Captive Nations: Eastern Europe, 1945-1990.* New York: Avon, 1990. [History of the region arranged by country.]

Dawisha, Karen. *Eastern Europe, Gorbachev and Reform: The Great Challenge.* New York: Cambridge University Press, 1990. [Provides the international background to the recent changes in Eastern Europe.]

Lomax, Bill. *The Hungarian Worker's Council in 1956.* New York: Columbia University Press, 1990. [Account of the Hungarian uprising of 1956.]

Magris, Claudio. *Danube. A Sentimental Journey from the Source to the Black Sea.* New York: Farrar Straus & Giroux, 1990. [Travelogue composed by a leading Italian specialist in the history and culture of Eastern Europe.]

Okey, Robin. *Eastern Europe 1740-1985; Feudalism to Communism.* Minneapolis, Minn.: University of Minnesota Press, 1987. [Broad introduction to the history of the region; the best so far available.]

Rothschild, Joseph. *Return to Diversity. A Political History of East Central Europe since since World War II.* New York : Oxford University Press, 1990. [Full historical account of the Communist period in Eastern Europe, arranged thematically.]

Rupnik, Jacques. *The Other Europe.* New York: Schocken Books, 1989. [Lively and readable account of Eastern Europe under Communist rule.]

———. *East Central Europe Between the Two World Wars.* Seattle: University of Washington Press, 1990. [An account of life in Eastern Europe between World Wars I and II.]

Shawcross, William. *Dubcek: Dubcek and Czechoslovakia 1918-90.* New York: Simon & Schuster, 1990. [Biography of the leader of the 1968 "Prague Spring."]

Stokes, Gale. *From Stalinism to Pluralism: A Documentary History of Eastern Europe since 1945.* New York: Oxford University Press, 1991. [Gives the most important documents relating to the consolidation and collapse of Communist power in Eastern Europe.]

Toranska, Teresa. *Them: Stalin's Polish Puppets.* New York: HarperCollins, 1988. [Revealing and sometimes frightening interviews with former leading Polish Communists.]

Books on the history of Eastern Europe After 1989

Ash, Timothy Garton. *We the People. The Revolution of '89 Witnessed in Warsaw, Budapest, Berlin and Prague.* New York: Random House, 1990. [Eyewitness account of the revolutions of 1989.]

Batt, Judy. *East Central Europe from Reform to Transformation.* New York: St. Martin's Press, 1991. [Account of postrevolutionary politics in Czechoslovakia, Hungary, and Poland.]

Glenny, Misha. *The Rebirth of History: Eastern Europe in the Age of Democracy.* New York: Viking Penguin, 1991. [Account of the first year after the fall of Communism .]

———. *The Fall of Yugoslavia: The Third Balkan War.* New York: Viking Penguin, 1993. [The first authoritative account of the civil war in Yugoslavia.]

Sword, Keith, ed. *The Soviet Takeover of the Polish Eastern Provinces.* New York: St. Martin's Press, 1991. [Account of the Soviet invasion of the region.]

Novels and literary works

Many novels have been written about the conflicts in Eastern Europe. Most are available in several paperback editions.

Havel, Vaclav. *Living in Truth.* [Collection of essays by former Czech dissident and president.]

Kundera, Milan. *The Unbearable Lightness of Being.* [Story set in Czechoslovakia against the background of the Soviet invasion of 1968.]

Wagner, Richard. *Exit: A Story.* [Moving account by an ethnic German from Romania of his journey to a new life in the Federal Republic of Germany.]

Films

Film was the principal medium of social and political criticism during the Communist period. Because of censorship, however, producers and scriptwriters frequently made their points obliquely and through the use of allegory. Eastern European films are not usually shown on television in the West, but if you live in or near a major city, you might find them playing at some movie theaters. You can also sometimes find Eastern European films on video. The following are, worth watching for:

Closely Observed Trains (1966). Made in Czechoslovakia, the film is set in a small railway station during World War II.

Danton (1983). Directed by Andrzej Wajda in France. Although dealing with an aspect of the French Revolution, the film is thought to be a complex allegory of the struggle between Lech Walesa (Danton) and President Jaruzelski (Robespierre).

Man of Iron (1981). Directed by Andrzej Wajda. A sequel to *Man of Marble*, the film is set against the background of the Solidarity-led strikes of 1980-1981. With the imposition of martial law in 1981, the film was banned in Poland.

Man of Marble (1976). Directed by Andrzej Wajda. The story of a Polish worker-hero in the 1950s who has a statue made in his honor. After running into trouble with the Communist authorities, he is imprisoned and the statue is removed.

Private Vice, Public Virtues (1976). Directed by the Hungarian Miklos Jancso and made in Italy. The film, which depicts a prince whose idealism gives way to sexual self-indulgence, is an allegory of the conflict in Hungary between socialism and consumerism.

INDEX

DATE			